For Jonah, Isaac and Eyra,
who all know the farm
where Joey was born – M.M.

To Kitty – T.C.C.

EGMONT

First published in Great Britain 2020 by Egmont Books UK Ltd
2 Minster Court, London EC3R 7BB
www.egmontbooks.co.uk
Text copyright © Michael Morpurgo 2020
Illustrations copyright © Tom Clohosy Cole 2020

The moral rights of Michael Morpurgo and Tom Clohosy Cole have been asserted.

ISBN 978 14052 9244 3
Printed in Italy
70090/001

A CIP catalogue record for this book is available from the British Library.

With thanks to Sarah Phillips at the British Horse Society and to Alan Wakefield and William Smith.

MICHAEL MORPURGO
WAR HORSE

Illustrated by
TOM CLOHOSY COLE

EGMONT

Joey and Albert were like brothers. Joey might have been a young farm horse, and Albert a young lad, but those two, they loved one another like brothers, more maybe. His mother and father said so, everyone in the village said so.

They grew up together on the family farm in the rolling hills of Devon. Albert only had to call Joey's name, whistle him up – hooting like an owl – and his horse would come running.

Together they would ride down the deep lanes to school, gallop like the wind over Candlelight Meadow, trot through Bluebell Wood and along the river, where the herons lifted off and the kingfisher flashed by and the salmon leapt. They ploughed and sowed in the fields, cut the grass for hay, harvested the corn, gathered in the sheep.

They worked hard, Joey and Albert, but their life was just about as perfect and happy, and peaceful, as it could be.

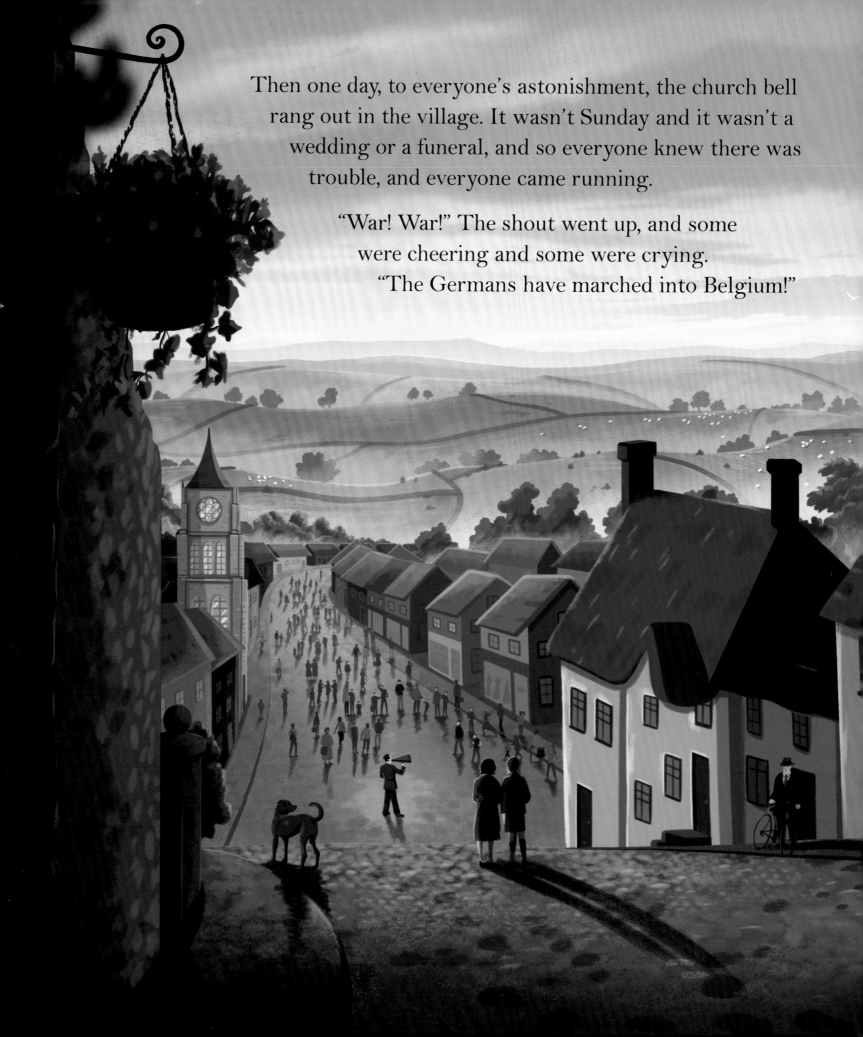

Then one day, to everyone's astonishment, the church bell rang out in the village. It wasn't Sunday and it wasn't a wedding or a funeral, and so everyone knew there was trouble, and everyone came running.

"War! War!" The shout went up, and some were cheering and some were crying. "The Germans have marched into Belgium!"

Albert didn't know much about Germany or Belgium.
All he knew was that they were faraway places, across
the sea. So any war, he thought, would be far away too.
"It's nothing to worry about, Joey," he said, as they
rode back home to the farm. "Life will go on just
the same. It'll all be over soon enough.
You and me, we'll be fine."

But Albert was wrong. He wasn't to know how long and terrible this war would be. He wasn't to know that the army would be needing horses, all the horses they could get: horses for the cavalry, horses to pull the carts and the guns, the ammunition wagons and the ambulances.

And Albert wasn't to know that, soon, his father would be badly in need of money, to keep the farm going and feed the family.

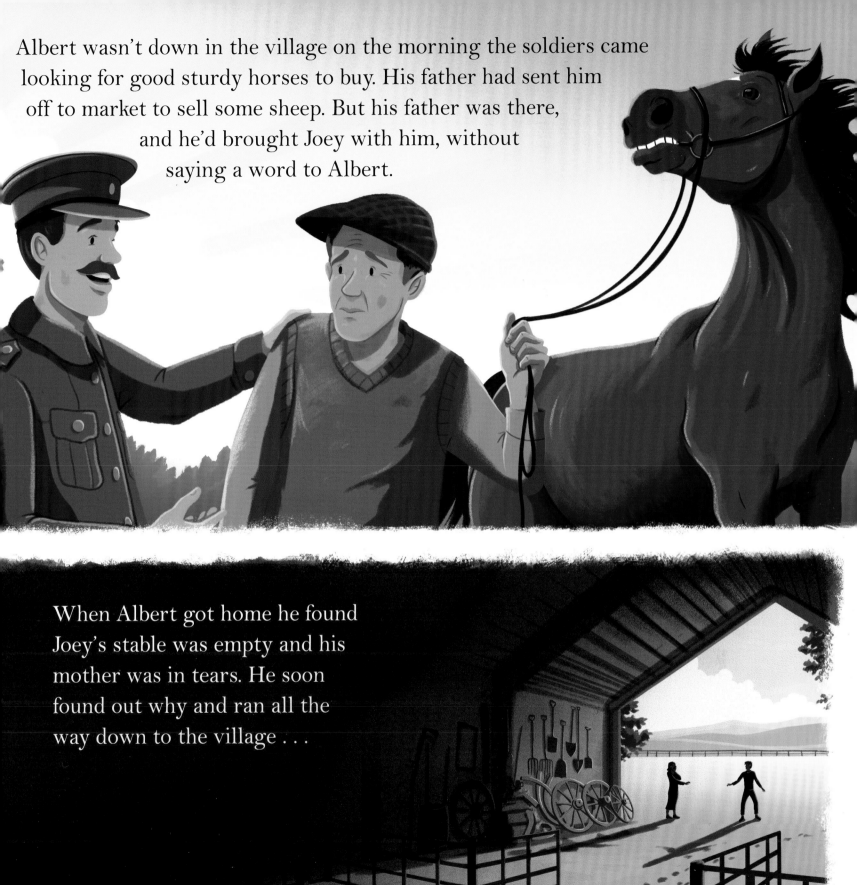

Albert wasn't down in the village on the morning the soldiers came looking for good sturdy horses to buy. His father had sent him off to market to sell some sheep. But his father was there, and he'd brought Joey with him, without saying a word to Albert.

When Albert got home he found Joey's stable was empty and his mother was in tears. He soon found out why and ran all the way down to the village . . .

But he was too late. Joey had already been sold to the army. Captain Nichols, the officer in charge, took Albert aside and tried to explain: "I'm afraid Joey belongs to the army now. But don't you worry, I'll take good care of him for you. Promise."

There was nothing more Albert could do. He put his arms around Joey and made him one last faithful promise. "I'll find you, Joey," he whispered. "I will. One day you'll hear me calling you like I always do, and you'll know it's me. Listen for me, Joey. I'll find you, I promise."

Back home, Albert packed his bag and said goodbye to his parents. "I shan't speak to you again, Father, not after what you've done," he said. "I may be too young, but I'm going to join up in the army. I'm going after Joey, and there's nothing you can do."

Of course, his mother did all she could to stop him, but Albert's mind was made up. He found the recruiting office, where he stood as tall as he could, spoke as deeply as he could, and told the sergeant that he was 18. "You look more like 15 or 16 to me," the sergeant said. "But we need all the soldiers we can get. So you'll do."

They gave Albert a uniform and a rifle, and boots that were too big for him and gave him blisters, and sent him off for training. They marched him up and down, taught him how to shoot straight and polish his buttons and boots. Finally he went to battle in far-off France. And all the while, he kept his eye out for his Joey.

Every horse he saw gave Albert new hope – but none of them was like Joey. His Joey was a shining red bay, with a black mane and tail. He had four perfectly matched white socks and a white cross on his forehead. There wasn't another horse like him.

Albert told his friends all about Joey, how he was going to find him if it was the last thing he did. "Then we'll go back home to England and be happy again. You'll see." But his friends, good pals, thought his search was hopeless, and they'd tease him about it sometimes. "There are thousands of horses! You'll never find him."

Albert's days as a soldier were mostly spent waiting, waiting
in the trenches with the rifle fire crackling and the whine of the
shells as they flew overhead, waiting to be sent up over the top
of the trenches and out across No Man's Land.

Huddled in his dugout, he kept saying to himself, "I'll find you, Joey, I will." Sometimes he found himself shouting it out loud. When he woke each morning, there was only one thought on his mind: to live through the day, so he could find his Joey.

Albert didn't know it, but his Joey was not more than a few miles away. He was a cavalry horse now, ridden by Captain Nichols. The captain had become very fond of him. He liked to draw pictures of Joey whenever he could, and he was taking good care of him, just as he had promised Albert he would.

As for Joey, he too dreamed of life back home, of happy days out in the fields with his Albert. And he too had a friend: a tall black stallion the soldiers called Topthorn. Topthorn was stabled next to him, and whenever they could, they grazed together, drank together, galloped side by side. They were a great comfort to one another.

But Joey and Topthorn could never forget
the war. Night and day, the guns roared and
the ground shook. There was little shelter from
the wind and rain, and there was never enough
food or water. Captain Nichols did his best for
them, came and talked to them often, especially
at night-time, when the shelling lit up the sky.
He smoothed their necks and calmed their
fears, told them all would be well.

But one day their lives would change completely. It was in the first cavalry charge of the war. Captain Nichols was riding Joey, charging with the troop through the smoke and noise of battle. Topthorn was galloping beside them. Suddenly Joey could feel that Captain Nichols was no longer on his back. His stirrups were swinging free. There were no other horses around him, except Topthorn, and Joey saw that he too had lost his rider. All around them there were soldiers in grey uniforms and helmets, speaking strangely. On the ground lay so many horses, so many men. Joey and Topthorn were caught and taken away.

Joey and Topthorn were in the German army now. But they weren't being used as cavalry horses any more – they were ambulance horses. Hitched up side by side to an ambulance cart, filled with wounded soldiers, they hauled the cart several miles from the battlefield to a field hospital on a farm.

They soon discovered that the German soldiers in their grey uniforms were just like the British soldiers in their khaki uniforms. They might speak differently, but, like the British, the Germans were tired and cold and hungry and frightened and longed to go home. Joey and Topthorn felt the same.

The work was hard, but the two friends were always together side by side as they pulled their ambulance. And when they came back each evening to the farm near the field hospital where they were stabled, a young girl and her grandfather would come and talk to them, and bring them fresh water and sweet-smelling hay.

When the summer came, and the fighting moved further away, Joey and Topthorn were not needed so often to fetch the wounded back from the trenches. Then the little girl would ride them on the farm. They felt safe with her. But still they longed for home. Every night Joey thought of his Albert, wondered where he was, every day he listened out for his call.

But their blissful days of peace and happiness did not last for long.
One autumn morning, they looked out of their stable to see a troop
of horse artillery coming down the dusty track. The officer in charge
strode over to them and looked them up and down. Before they knew
it, Joey and Topthorn were dragged into the farmyard and hitched up
to a gun team with four other horses. They were war horses again,
this time pulling guns.

The autumn turned to winter. Day in, day out, Joey and Topthorn hauled guns down long roads, up rutty hills, through sinking mud. Every day was more exhausting than the last. They were driven hard, shouted and cursed at, sometimes whipped. The work and the cold and mud took their strength. Joey could see that Topthorn was not well. He took longer to stand up each morning, and he was limping badly.

But one morning, they found themselves being led away from the guns by another soldier, older than the rest. He was kinder to them than the others had been. "Hello, you lovely horses," he said. "I am Friedrich Muller. Do not worry, I shall look after you as if you were my children. I have children, you know, back home in Germany. Four of them, all girls. It's all I want, to go home to my family."

And Friedrich was as good as his word. He did treat Joey and Topthorn
like his own children. There were no more whips, no more shouting
and cursing, just the gentleness and kindness of their friend Friedrich.
Topthorn was still weak, still limping, but he was happier in his spirits
now. The loads of ammunition they had to pull were not too heavy,
Friedrich made sure of that. They stopped often for rest and water,
and Friedrich sang to them, the songs he sang to his children back
home. Listening to him calmed their fears.

One day, they were resting in a wood. Friedrich was sitting down under a tree, singing, whilst the two horses drank from the stream. The shelling came quite suddenly. The whole wood seemed to be exploding around them. There were fires everywhere. The horses tried to run, but Topthorn lost his footing and fell. Joey waited beside him. But Topthorn didn't get up. Friedrich tried to help him, but Topthorn lay still, not moving, not breathing.

Friedrich saw there was nothing more he could do, and he tried to pull Joey away. But Joey would not leave his old friend's side. The shelling went on and on all around them. Too late Friedrich tried to run. He fell and lay still.

Joey stayed there for hours beside his Topthorn. The shelling stopped. But then another terrible noise echoed through the trees, a rattling and roaring sound.

Tanks – like great metal monsters they were! And they were rumbling over the stream, coming straight towards him. Terrified, Joey ran, ran and ran. As darkness fell around him, he galloped though fields and farmyards, through ruined villages.

He stumbled into craters, tripped into barbed wire, and jumped trenches. He had no idea where he was going. He was just running, running for his life. On and on he went, until his legs hurt him so much, he could run no more.

Albert was half asleep on sentry duty in his trench, when he saw something move in No Man's Land. He raised the alarm. Soon the trenches were full of soldiers, helmets on, rifles at the ready, expecting an attack. Albert's sergeant was beside him. "What is it?" he asked Albert. "What d'you see?"

"I think it's a horse, Sarge. There's a horse out there in No Man's Land."

There was laughing all around from his pals. One of them said: "Albert's always seeing horses, Sarge. It'll be his Joey. He never stops looking for him." And they all laughed again.

But then they heard excited voices from the German trenches opposite: "Ein Pferd! Ein Pferd!"

"That means horse," someone called out. "They've seen it too!"

And another voice. "A white flag! Don't shoot! One of them's climbing up out of their trenches. He's going to fetch the horse."

Albert knew already, in his heart of hearts, that the horse had to be his Joey. And before anyone could stop him he was up and out of the trench, clambering through the barbed wire, and walking out into the mud of No Man's Land towards the horse and the German soldier with the white flag, who was already close by.

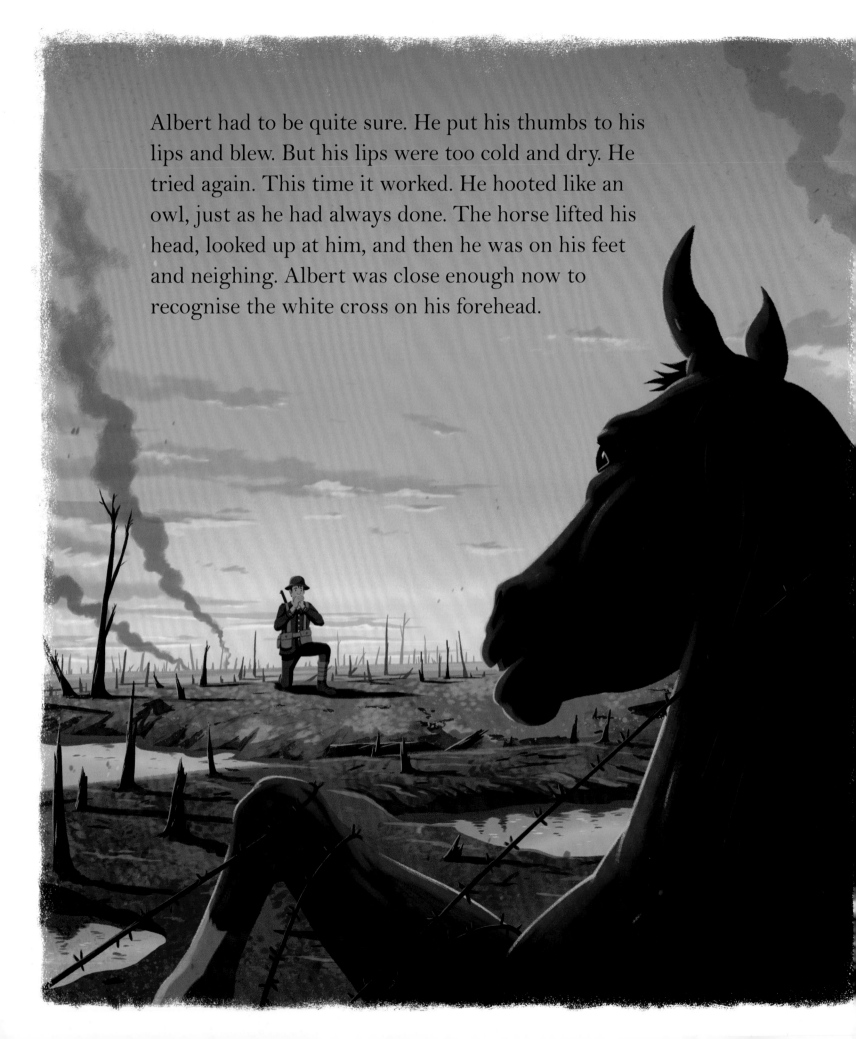

Albert had to be quite sure. He put his thumbs to his lips and blew. But his lips were too cold and dry. He tried again. This time it worked. He hooted like an owl, just as he had always done. The horse lifted his head, looked up at him, and then he was on his feet and neighing. Albert was close enough now to recognise the white cross on his forehead.

The two soldiers met in the middle of No Man's Land, the horse between them. "This is my Joey, my horse from home," said Albert. "Do you speak English?"

"Of course. I learned it in my school," the soldier replied. "And I have to say that, as I was here first, he is my horse."

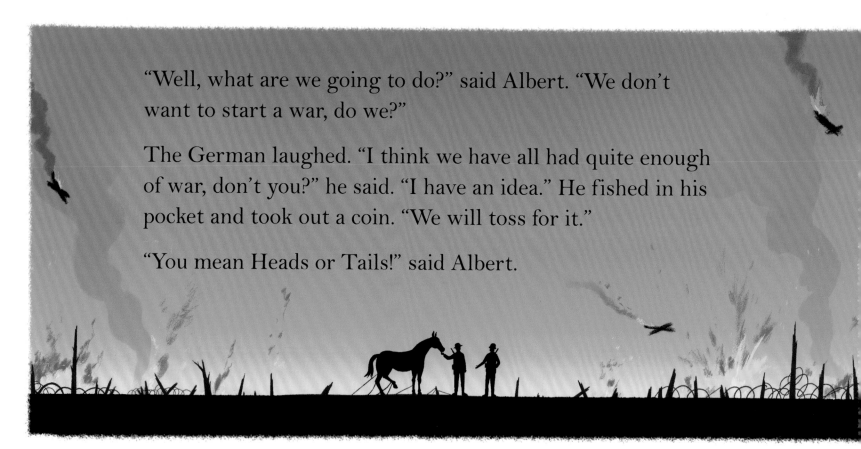

"Well, what are we going to do?" said Albert. "We don't want to start a war, do we?"

The German laughed. "I think we have all had quite enough of war, don't you?" he said. "I have an idea." He fished in his pocket and took out a coin. "We will toss for it."

"You mean Heads or Tails!" said Albert.

Joey came closer, and rested his head on Albert's shoulder. Albert put his arm around his neck and Joey nickered softly into his ear. He knew that, win or lose, Joey would have no choice.

"All right," Albert said. "You toss, I'll call."

The German soldier tossed. And Albert called out, "Heads!"

The coin spun high into the air, and seemed to take forever to fall. The German soldier bent down, picked it up, wiped off the mud, and then after a long pause, he looked up and said, "I am afraid this is the face of my Kaiser, my king, looking up at me, and he does not look pleased. The horse is yours."

He handed Albert the reins. Then he held out his hand. Albert took it. They clasped hands tight for a long moment and looked one another in the eye. Albert was searching his head for the words. "Auf Wiedersehen," he said. "Danke schön."

The soldier smiled. "So you do speak German!"

"Just goodbye and thank you," Albert told him.

"I think I do not need to tell you this," the German soldier said, "but look after this horse. I know you will, because I believe you, about this being your horse from home. He knew you, I could see that. Take him safely back home."

"And was it really Heads?" Albert asked him as he walked away.

The German waved his white flag in the air, and laughed. "You will never know," he said. "You will never know."

And so, a few months later, when the war was over, when Joey was stronger again, they came home together, riding down into the village. The flags were out, the church bells were ringing, the band was playing. There was a banner up over the village green: 'Welcome home, Albert. Welcome home, Joey. Welcome Peace.'

WELCOME PEACE

Albert and his father made their peace too. And life went on as before. Albert and Joey ploughed and sowed the fields together, reaped and mowed . . .

. . . and they rode again through Bluebell Wood, and along the river, and saw the herons and the kingfishers. The seasons came and went, and all was well.

And Albert went on all his life
wondering who that German
soldier was, and whether it really
had been Heads or Tails.